SHORT TALES UNFOLDED

KJP ALLEN

SHORT TALES UNFOLDED

Typesetting and cover design by FormattingExperts.com

STORIES

DEDICATION

Thanks to the One above who continues to instill the inspirations, the motivation, and the creativity, to bring to life new styles of writing. A special appreciation to Rafael and his Team for making another Journey continue onto new Paths. To Ms. Aleah W for diligently elevating my writing levels and helping to make them shine brighter. Ms. Meza for her deep insights and uplifting references: Ms. McMahon for her guidance and to all those who supported me on my first book: I will be Forever Grateful. May you all continue to be delighted with the stories. Included is a piece by my (young) sister.

THE JUDGE

For a long time, I wanted to tell you that I was a Judge in the Courts. I engaged in Civil and Family Cases. Not on a large scale and not like you think. No one knew of my title and the cases in which I presided over. I was not at liberty to share the proceedings while the cases were in session. The JUDGES strict codes were – No public audiences and No discussions regarding cases that anyone took. I am sorry that you were not aware of my position, please forgive me. You can call me an "Undercover Judge Judy."

Did I take the Bar Exam, you want to know? No, I did not take it. The bar was too high, the cost too much, and I was not a selected member of the inner circle of judges. In addition, the time to get my degree was too long.

Being a Judge and presiding over cases came naturally to me. My career started out at the youthful age of six. As you can see, I have been around for a long time. I presided over international and local Juvenile and Adult Cases and the caseloads began to increase.

The elation of conducting my role as a judge was one of joy. I began to Listen and hear more cases on the Family Level. '*To be a good Judge, one had to be impartial,*' I said to myself. The appeals within those cases were easier to observe with the evidence, and the Families needed a Fair and Honest Judge on their side in the courts.

I used my expertise from the bench and used it wisely outside the court room. This was a prime example why I approached my judging with more scrutiny. For instance, when individuals travelled years ago, they dressed as though they were attending a formal function. Fancy hats and dresses for the ladies and suits and ties for the men. Travelers today parade on the plane in their pyjamas, and shorts and beach slippers. They are thinking to themselves, '*What was there to do on a plane except to sit or go to sleep. Why not be comfortable?*'

My Judging outside of the court room surfaced when I was attending a 7:30 Church Mass. As service began, a man silently glided into the pew four rows ahead of me. Would you believe that he was in a rumpled torn shirt, raggedy shorts with holes in the pockets, and a dented helmet under his arm?

'Judge the man,' my inner mind shouted.

'Sentence him. Have him leave the pews at once,' my second ego declared.

My outside of the court verdict was, *'Why in the world would a person come to service dressed as he was and sit up front?'* You should have seen me ready to pound my fist (*I had no gavel*) on the bench in front of *me* and throw my prayer book at him declaring out loud, ***"Dismissed from the room."***

I wanted to berate him and say, *'Do not let me see you in this place again.'*

It was tempting to stroll up to his pew where he sat and make a motion to the preacher to have him thrown out of the church, like you would when addressing a case inside the courts.

Suddenly I shook myself out of my make-believe courtroom fantasy and thought, *'He may not have good clothes to wear, or he did not want to miss Service that day or he just needed to pray.'* Silly of me, applying my Court Room sentences and I was not on duty. I was declaring him unfit to enter the church. I was Judging and implicating the man. I was judging his clothing as not appropriate. That was my first Strike!

A couple of weeks later, my Judging approach showed itself again. I went running and hurried into a store to pick up supplies for work. This time I was in a jogging suit not in a judge's robe. Realizing, that I was not going to make it home in time to dress, I snuck quietly into Church for the late Mass.

REMEMBER that I was out for a run, I had my shopping supplies, and I was in my running suit. I cowered in the back pew in a corner seat, not to be visible to the congregation. As I knelt to pray, memories FLOODED BACK to me FAST and FURIOUS. I WAS GUILTY on all accounts! Accusing and sentencing a man two weeks ago in church for his dress code, while I was doing a similar faux pas. Would you believe that I was on trial within myself? Did I not learn my lessons you may wonder?

Not so, as you continue to read. Late one night, I returned from a competitive event and slithered like a snake into a Huge Church when I walked out of the Subway to the musical sound of Handel's Messiah filtering through my ears. Hearing the music stimulated my mind reminding me of an assignment for my music course in college. The written paper was due the following week. The assignment was to attend a show which included a classical style genre, depicted musical cadences with upbeat tempos, and a variety of instruments.

That was strike two for me.

Realization of my faulty ways again exploded in my mind so forcefully I thought I had a migraine. That made me pray a little longer to ask forgiveness: Why? I was in an athletic attire not appropriate for Church, and I had Judged others without a license. Just I had Judged the man for his shabby clothing in Church for which I did the similar thing, not ONCE but TWICE. That was hypocritical of me. This is when I hung up my Robe.

It was time to retire. It was time to give up my Judges' license, give up my caseloads, and leave the bench behind me. My reason: For Judging cases under false pretences. What one witnesses and visibly observe, is not always what it appears to be.

Do not Judge others so hastily least they Judge you in return unfairly.

ALL OR NONE

No one returns home alone when you left together as a group. Safety of the group strengthened in numbers. It was about leaving out together and returning home together. Families have ingrained the rule and passed it down from generation to generation as a way of keeping children safe. Darlene did not follow that line of tradition and chose to be alone when it came to going home one day.

School was over for that day and Darlene and her classmates were going home in separate directions, and she was hungry. Gurgling noises began coming from her tummy drowning out the birds that were chirping from the trees. That may be the reason for her being alone as she frolicked merrily and as her hands swayed back and forth, and her feet skipped as if she was jumping rope at recess. She wondered what was there to eat for a snack. She had not eaten lunch.

Upon arriving home, she greeted her *Gran-Aunt* and was about to skip her way into her room to change out of her school uniform before heading into the kitchen for her snack. Before she entered the room she heard, "*Where is your cousin Paul?*"

Sharply turning around on her heels like a thrower in the throwing circle, Darlene thought to herself, *'How should I know? Do you see him?'* Instead, she replied, "*I do not know.*" It was the wrong answer.

Her *Gran-Aunt*'s hands were akimbo as she spoke, "*Find him, and do not come back home until you are both together.*"

Darlene, looked blankly at her as to say, *'Where should I look for a boy after school? Gran-Aunt* kept staring at her without blinking.

Darlene blinked and paused: she queried in her mind? Had she missed the lecture in the morning before school or did her *Gran-Aunt* forgot to mention it before she and Paul left for school. Or was she was not listening at all?

Adults expect children to complete certain tasks: for instance, making up their beds or taking out the rubbish. On occasions the directions are not clear or fully explained. Or the adult who told the child to complete a task forgot to tell the child in the first place!

Darlene saw the look, (DO not be smart with me) on her *Gran-Aunt*'s face. She hesitated, considered her next move, did an about militant face turn, and marched back out the door. Thinking to herself, *'Which direction would Paul be coming from?'* The steep hill they both walked down to school that morning was not the path they usually walked to return home. Maybe if you were a mountain climber you would climb back up that hill! Paul had to be coming home by the long route. Typical of a boy and idling no doubt!

Darlene shuffled her steps and dragged her feet in irritation at not eating her snack and meandered back the long way. Luckily, she spied Paul playing marbles with the boys in someone's yard.

She trotted and increased her steps towards the boys and grabbed Paul by his shirt. Yanking him up so that he was on his tippy-toes she angrily said, "Get yourself away from the marbles and come home right-away."

Struggling and pulling his shirt from Darlene, Paul screamed, "Not going with you." Paul was not in the mood for her pulling him away from the game that he was winning.

"NO. You are coming with me this instance or else I am throwing your marbles into the bushes," as she grabbed a hand full of the marbles out of the circle on the ground.

Ready to throw them, Paul pleads, "Please, no. Please stop. I will go," as he lowers his head and sulkily follows her home.

Darlene was fretting nervously as both of them left the yard and headed home. She was taking no chances as she shoved Paul along in-front of her each step he took. She missed her snack as her tummy was noisily reminding her at the moment.

"Stop pushing me. Do you not see I am walking? Stop pushing I said," as they both moved along the road.

Internally Darlene's mind was thinking, '*He was going to get into trouble when they reached home. I cannot wait. I bet you Gran-Aunt would not allow him to ride the new bike we got for Christmas.*' Upon entering the house, her *Gran-Aunt* looked at Darlene, ignored Paul, and said, "Did I not say to you this morning as I always do, if you leave this house together, you must come back home together?"

"You children do not listen. You ignore safety rules."

How was Darlene to know of that GOLDEN RULE? *Gran-Aunt* did not say such a thing that morning; but to cross her, would have been unwise. Darlene's only answer to give was, "*I just forgot.*"

To that reply, her *Gran-Aunt* remarked, "*Do not let it happen again,*" and walked away.

Her *Grand-Aunt* did not give Paul any recognition or talking to. He did not get reprimanded. Was he a lucky boy? Was he being Gran-Aunt's favourite, or she was saving his reprimand for another day? Paul flashed his teethy smile at Darlene and scampered outside.

Darlene seethed with frustration inside of her. Why was she the only one chastised when they were both wrong. It was nothing that she could have done about how Grand-Aunt made her feel. Darlene was angry at Paul and mad at her *Gran-Aunt.*

She wondered again, '*When did her Gran-Aunt say for both of them to leave together and come back together?*' She hurried outside and grabbed Paul before he could squeal for help. "Did you know that we both were to return home at the same time?" He shrugged his shoulders and grinned that toothy smile again and did not utter a word.

Darlene pushed him away and tried to recall in her mind the events in her day. Nothing came to her thoughts about hearing the RULE. *Was she supposed to figure out the subliminal message that her Gran-Aunt had not spoken?*

That day she Learned the Golden Rule about leaving together and returning together. Implied Rules learned at home were not Taught in School.

DARKNESS

Suddenly, it was completely DARK in the apartment. No one was visible. Screaming and yelling and wailings sounded from outside.

"What's going on. What happened to the lights? I cannot see a thing. Did the fuse go out? Where are you?" Your mom was nervously speaking to no one in particular.

Cherrie heard your dad yelling, "*Where is the flashlight. Will Someone get me a flashlight?*"

Cherrie was in the Living room, and frantically felt for the wall that headed towards the passageway to get her bearings that lead to the supply closet. Could you imagine her trying to navigate in the dark to find the flashlight? Fumbling clumsily with the doorknob of the closet in the dark, she eventually rummaged in the drawers where she remembered she saw the flashlights. She found two flashlights: pushed the switch on and off three times, making sure the battery was working as she scanned the area with the bright beam on, and headed back towards the living room.

Zigzagging the beam of light along her path she located your parents. One flashlight she gave to your dad and the other she shone outside while peeking through the blinds.

Only the parked cars and people moving about like ghosts she saw from her concealed spot.

"Get away from that window," your mother said. "Do you want the people to break in and take our flashlights?"

Macon city had plunged into darkness. 'BLACKOUT, BLACKOUT, it is a BLACKOUT,' Cherrie heard scared and confused voices coming from somewhere outside.

Suddenly a loud crash echoed as if someone had broken a glass window.

"You hear that sound? Do you hear them breaking into the cars to steal things while no one can see them? Do you want to be a witness in the police station as an accomplice to their looting?" Spouted your mother, while rubbing her huge belly. "Who knows what they would do to us, seeing that we are on the first floor already. Get away from the window, NOW."

What a time for the Blackout to take place. Your mom was pregnant with you. You were due at any time. Cherrie was thinking, "*What if your mom went into labour? Would your dad be able to drive to the hospital? Everything was Black, Black, Black.*"

More screaming coming from the outside. Cherrie shone her flashlight around and into your mom's face. She looked worried with her eyes bulging like a Deer in flashlights.

Recollections of the nursing training raced through Cherrie's mind. To prepare the girls for life skills, Midwives trained them to be helpers because no schools were available. A practice which was critical and appropriate for the girls no matter where they lived. Cherrie learning was due to the training she received when she lived in the hills of Renard long ago.

Females of the Renard community had the responsibility of passing down the knowledge and traditions to the younger girls. The Midwives essential life lessons and wisdom proved beneficial for all females. Cherrie remembered the noises of the mothers in labour were loud and vocal. *How could one escape* **those screams** coming from their mouths during labour in the nursing centers or in their homes? Every young girl witnessed pregnant mothers entering a birthing location with heavy burdens inside their bodies and leaving lighter by carrying their precious bundles in arms was a common sight. Therefore, Cherrie was emotionally ready in her mind. She went over the drills that she memorized:

- Wash hands – *They had to be clean.*
- Boil water – *to sterilize the utensils.*
- Find clean towels – *To wrap the newborn.*
- Find clean sheets – *For the mother to lay on.*
- Scissors – *to cut the umbilical cord.*

Cherrie knew the process by rote. *Past knowledge was the key to maintaining the traditions. Keeping calm and level-headed was to be in control of any situation.*

She went through the next phase of the drills:

Breathe in Breathe out. Again.

Breathe in. Breathe out. Again

Breathe in. Breathe out.

She could do this.

Cherrie checked with your mother again and asked, "*Are you OK?*"

Your mother replied, "*Yes.*"

Cherrie did not think your mother was, OK.

With unknown images of what was going on outside and the pressures of what could happen inside the apartment at any moment, she wondered: *'Would she get the items quickly for the birthing of the baby with just a flashlight? Would using the candles be better than holding a flashlight while preparing for the birthing?'*

As fast as she thought of the second solution, *'The fear of fire being ignited caused by lit candles intensified within her along with the tensions in the room.'* She fidgeted as she searched around with the flashlight to locate the candles and matches.

By the time she lit the candles and the room ablaze with light, your father's hair looked a shade whiter. He was a nervous wreck. He certainly was. It was too soon for your arrival date.

His eyes said it all:

What if you had arrived earlier than expected in the apartment?

Would he manage with no nurses or doctors?

Would your mother control her nerves?

Would it be a long-drawn-out birth?

Would she be able to deal with the pain?

Would he bear the screaming?

Cherrie's mind analyzed and surveyed the two adults. She knew that her knowledge of helping the midwives with childbirth was still intact. Even though it was awhile back since she saw a child being born, no refresher course was necessary. Should the feet or the crown appear first, there was a set routine. *'What if your mother went hysterical?'*

How hard could this be now that she was older to deliver a baby? Cherrie had no time to let negativity run through her mind. There was a situation at hand and being level-headed was the advice she gave herself.

The planned birthing was down to a **D-Delivery**.

The Anxious waiting for daylight along with the loud breaking of glass outside had Carrie wondering if you would make your appearance. That prevented her from sleeping. She also would have been a nuisance if she constantly asked over and over was your mom OK. Therefore, she quietly laid down in the dark alone leaving your mom with your dad. Carrie's mind was like a roller coaster out of control. Thoughts flooded her mind:

Birth in Blackout – what would they have named you?

Would your mom make it through the night with no contractions?

When would there be power in the city?

Jubilation at daybreak for the apartment trio as natural daylight peeked in. Everyone made it as the morning arrived. There no still no power as it had been the night before. We were all worried about you in the DARK, inside your mom. However, you on the other hand waiting on the inside was oblivious to what was happening on the outside. You remained comfortable in the womb letting chaos wreak havoc outside.

'You were the smart one by staying in the dark.' Why come out of your **dark place** to more **darkness**? You were not ready to face the mess: ***And what a mess it was!***

LESSON LEARNED

A fresh start to his Ryan's young adulthood. The journey on which he was about to embark upon he had never travelled before. He alone was the navigator. He was the controller. He was the expert in his own fate. He was to attend a State University, not the Alma Mater of which the males in his family attended.

Ryan was to begin his college career at a Radcliff State University. Would he feel out of place and awkward?

He thought to himself, 'How difficult could it be to attend the classes he selected and begin the new term?' He had much to learn, which he found out very soon. Faith deemed it not to be as Ryan wanted. Three days before his metamorphosis from youth to adult the **College Board** of Radcliff University had the audacity to send a letter informing him of the increase in tuition fees for his entire semester. The price had tripled from when he received his acceptance letter. The quoted fees the College initially transcribed was not the same when Ryan's second letter arrived.

There was no way Ryan could envision paying the inflated cost. His vision for something new in his life seemed doomed. Just when he thought that he would be the one to break the tradition of the same old City College, the possibility was no longer available.

He knew that his father would not pay the additional funding. Especially with Ryan not wanting to attend the family Alma Mater initially.

Ryan's father was under the assumption that the College Freshman Committee had paid the entire payment for four years. He did not want to tell his father that he needed money for tuition so close the start of the semester. City College no longer offered open enrollment as it did when his Dad and brothers attended in the past.

Ryan was in the new era: all students had to pay for their courses. The money he saved working the summer jobs was just enough to pay for books. He could no longer attend Radcliff University.

Ryan was so disappointed at not being able to attend the University, he left the house and walked and walked for hours. Facing the reality that he must choose the College that his brothers attended, saddened him more. What did a first-year student know about college except what his father and brothers told him?

Would the choices in his first year as an incoming student, reflect on his life four years from now? Ryan wanted to make his own decisions as to what he studied and not what his father and brothers thought he should study.

Frustration, uncertainty, and insecurity bombarded Ryan and clogged his mind. Was he too late to register and add his name into the family's Alma Marta history?

Would they accept him for the Fall semester with classes soon to begin?

Ryan did not select any of the City Colleges as an alternative choice on his application. Now that he had no other choice but to attend the City College his brothers and dad raved about, and he was afraid that he had missed the enrollment deadline.

There went his dreams of going away to a State Radcliff *University.*

There went his hopes for being the independent brother, the one that wanted to leave, and the one that did not break the cycle.

He reflected on the orientation festival he attended, and how excited he was to be attending the Fall Semester on his own away from home at Radcliff University.

Disenchanted and devastated, he perked up before allowing disappointment to ruin his transition from youth to adult independence.

He wanted no help from his father like his brothers had done before him. It was his life to plan on his own. He was determined to make it work to his advantage.

Ryan felt like he was swimming up and down the stream blindly with no direction and no guidance when he entered the enrollment office at City College the next day.

What was he getting himself into alone with no financial help? He shrugged and walked into the so-called registration room.

Long Lines, paper all over the floor, rows of consoles with numbers up in front, and no place to sit. Nervous, unsure, and confused of knowing that he could not back out of attending college, he forged ahead.

College was to a given norm in the family.

College degrees provided more opportunities in life. Often, Ryan was reminded he had to get a College degree.

A booming voice jarred Ryan from his rationalizing:

> Freshman students:
>
> "You must complete the financial aid form and return it to window number ONE if you are not paying with cash or a check or a credit card. Tear off the front of the form which explains the aid. Read it carefully and sign the back and print your full name."
>
> Second: *"Take a booklet and six cards from the back table and make your selections. Create several class schedules and then bring your choices up to the front consoles."*

The time was nine o'clock in the morning and Ryan slowly turned his head to see where the voice was emitting from, as he picked up a booklet. ***The voice was a Big Guy behind the glass window.*** Glancing at the booklets, Ryan immediately completed the financial form. He read the front page and noticed the waiver for extending first semester deadline payments until April. His luck was beginning to be in his favour.

He moved forward enthusiastically with the selection of courses for the semester with renewed vigour and chose the maximum eighteen credits recommended. In about an hour, Ryan had five cards with a variety of selections. '*Not bad he thought.*' He approached the consoles, handed in the cards, took a number, and waited. To his surprise, after only waiting for one minute he heard his number announced.

Ryan was hoping for a class schedule confirmation on one of the selected cards he completed. Short lived elation. None of the cards had a perfect 100% class match in all columns. The Big Guy person behind the glass placed a check to the left of the classes that were still available. Ryan had to go back to the drawing board, so to say and fill in the unchecked classes with new classes that were available. Ryan thought, *'how could the classes be not available? It is not like they had pre-registration on-line.'*

By the time he figured out a suitable schedule and classes that pleased him, it was **one** o'clock. Ryan expected the card would be the one. To his astonishment, the cards were handed back. Ryan was advised by the tech attendant, "Two mandatory orientation courses were required by first-year students in order for the registration process to be completed."

"That was ridiculous," he said out aloud.

The Voice he heard at the beginning, **the Big Guy** up front, will not sign off until he added the two extra courses for one credit each. Ryan was fuming, tired, and irritable. It was close to 3 o'clock. The tech attendant suggested the two classes he needed to coincide best with no conflicts to his other classes. With two adjustments, the organized card was complete. At last, he had his card signed, and his schedule was complete. He submitted his CODED CARD to the console machine and completed the process. Ryan sullenly dragged himself home in relief, only to remember that classes would begin the following day.

First course of the day was the first-year mandatory class. Ryan's assignment: Transcribe an essay on his first day's experience in College for the next class meeting. He was very eager to complete his assignment.

He had first-hand knowledge of the first day experience fresh in his mind. When he received the grade for his assignment the next week in class, it was a **C grade.** Could you believe he got a C! Ryan was speechless and bitterly shocked at receiving a C grade. He overheard as a classmate whispering, 'First semester students with concerns about their low grades are allowed conferences with the professors to discuss the marks.'

Ryan decided, *'Why not just do that.'* He took his chances and made an appointment with the professor.

The professor mentioned to him, 'The assignment was not what she expected.'

Ryan spoke to the professor and asked, "What was needed to get his **'C'** grade to improve."

The professor replied, "Elaborate with more details and expand with concrete evidence on what the assignment asked of the writer."

Ryan said, "The details and instructions were unclear."

The professor intoned, **"The next class is your chance *to improve.*"**

The following assignment by the professor, Ryan received his grade. What had inspired Ryan to give him the courage to inquire about his grades the second week of school? He was not prepared for the shock the following week. The grade on his paper was a red D-.

Before the professor walked away from his desk, he braved and questioned why he received such a Low Score. The professor whispered, "It was an atrocious paper. The topic of assignment was to Write about whether it was better to 'Love and Lost than not to Love at All.' You Sir, missed the entire point of the topic."

Ryan had written about himself in love rather than all things in life. The BOLD RED writing on his paper suggested that he did not present enough comparisons to support both sides of the topic. It was a one-sided paper. This time he ignored the whispers about going to the professor for another grade check conference.

Ryan wondered why his grades were going backwards. *'This was not high school. College was an avenue to learn and grow. He had his future to create. It was only the beginning. He had to take charge.'* Ryan's second required student orientation course, was an advisory class. In the class, he learned new methods on how to manage obstacles that hindered his progress in his young life. He dealt with a variety of solutions and adjusted his approach to college classes.

Keeping a decent Grade Point Average, involved learning to move forward by comprehending the mistakes of the past. Ryan read, 'How to Books' to improve his essay writings. He used the suggestions as a guide to complete his assignments in all of his classes.

Ryan focused on the words the professors lectured in the classes and implemented the correct methods to improve his grades. He shook off the negative feelings and created a memorable first year.

Instead of allowing his grades to go from C to D to F, ***he applied and improved his learning styles: worked diligently to B where he should Be heading, which was the way to A better semester.***

I SAW YOU

Brilliant sunshine surrounded the day. With the clean smell in the air after the night's rainfall along with the warmth from the sun made it perfect morning for a brisk walk. While power walking through the neighbourhood and listening to my friend on the phone, I looked up ahead on the steep incline which I was about to ascend; Whom do I see?

You – The Lady – pushing a four-wheeler down a 60-degree incline on the footpath. You were coming down the hill too fast and not taking any notice of me as I watched you.

What happened? I decided to try and help.

I – Rushed forward making sure she did not have a runaway calamity.

The Lady – Barely moving – tip-toe, tip-toeing, on her wobbly legs.

I – Reached out to keep her steady realizing that her four-wheeler was teeter tottering, and she was about to fall.

The Lady – Shaking her head and bobbing it up and down trying to navigate the steep foot-path. (*I was uncertain whether the swaying of her head going back and forth was saying no or she was nervous* from my helping approach.)

I – Motioning with my palms held up in a stop sign, I tried to slow her down and offered to help balance the four-wheeler.

The dilemma? She was from a different Ethnic group. I was facing a Language barrier; and she was not responding to me.

The Lady – Brushed me off with her thin wavey arms going left and right.

Was it a No! Or was it a do not help me signal?

I – Panicked as she tried to control the four-wheeler's increasing speed down the steep foot-path.

Another dilemma: Which dialect should I begin with first? ***Chinese? Mandarin? Korean? Cantonese?***

I recalled a huffy rebuff I encountered with a female when I spoke in Korean. She told me - WRONG PERSON. Thus, remembering the past incident, I became hesitant. My Chinese greeting was first – "Do you need me to help," I questioned to the lady?

The Lady – Lifted her hands off the four-wheeler and spoke.' ***It sounded like Cantonese. Oh no!*** It was not Chinese she was muttering rapidly under her mask.

I – Speaking in what I thought was her language did not help with the communication. I tried to help guide the four-wheeler without touching her and walking ahead with my hands blocking her as if to prevent her from passing the speed limit.

The Lady – Brushed me off once more. Guiding her four-wheeler like a traffic controller at the airport to the level where the road plateaued.

I – Still concerned with her progress, I tried again to translate what she was garbling under her mask. The sounds I heard, and thought was not understandable. *Could it be that I made an error in thinking the language was Cantonese?* Was it another dialect I did not understand?

She had the audacity to try and cross the street without looking when she got to the levelled area. A stubborn lady, she was. The four-wheeler had no brakes. ***Applying a little Mandarin, I tried to speak to her and hoped she would slow down.*** She did not change her pace. She only seemed to move faster.

The Lady – Pushed the four-wheeler into the street in front of a car driving down the hill not thinking or acknowledging my feeble attempts of talking or helping. She was not concerned about what was going on around her. She was about her own business as if to say, SHE ***had everything in control.***

I – Stepping out cautiously I boldly stopped the car while simultaneously trying to direct her across the street. Waving to the driver, I continued my walk. However, I was still concerned about the lady as I glanced back watching her on the other side of the road on unsteady legs holding on to the fence meandering towards the benches.

How could a person at her age, make it down the steep slope on unsteady feet, driving a walker with no brakes, and not fall?

She had to have had an Angel sitting on her shoulders and watching over her.

On my second loop around the block, I entered that path where I saw the lady shielded by the fence. What a sight! There she was, sitting on the bench, eating her ***Curds and Whey*** *with a serene smile on her face, enjoying the shade.* Should I have worried? Not at all.

The Lady seemed to have had an agenda: LUNCH**!**

WILL THEY EVER CHANGE?

The older they become the more set in their ways they are. That is what lead to the phrase **Stubborn as a Mule**. No matter what you do or what you may say, the old timers want to have it their way. It is their way of doing things or else you are against them. When you try to speak to them, they shut you out of their lives forcing you to eventually bend to make them happy. As a result, they win no matter what.

James's father turned off his nine-to-five-time clock for two weeks. Dad's plan: a long-needed family trip. He desired to unwind and slow-down from the constant go, go, go, and get rest, and rest, and more rest. They packed and were on our way to the country for peace and quiet, fresh air and the beautiful scenery. Dad confirmed a stay at a bed and breakfast Town House in Fairville on the outskirts of town.

With just days to go, pondering about the quiet expanse and sights of endless land and trees, was enough to relax James' mind. The family wanted to leave the present concerns behind. A time to recharge and face the music (as the saying goes). He was not certain how does one face the music, seeing that James could not sing.

Do you want to know the thing or two about families returning to their family roots? They have this custom of visiting older relatives and the so-called extended family. The extended family are the individuals who are third and fourth cousins. There was a reason Dad made his visits and rounds at the beginning of his Vacation. Those reasons will reveal themselves in the next few chapters.

The following day after dad and the family got situated, they forged ahead with no special person in mind to make the so-called rounds. As ancient as those older folks looked, they knew when you arrived in town, who you dwelled with and when you were departing, without telephones in their homes. Unbelievable and scary.

James and his family passed by the Fairville market (it was Saturday) and whom should they see sitting in the main stall? *Ms. Know-it-all.* There was no avoiding her from her vantage point at the market's entrance. James entered the market and he pretended to touch the home-grown tomatoes when standing in front of her table filled with a variety of neatly grown vegetables.

"Good morning Ms. K," James said. "*Your garden had a bountiful season. These vegetables appear hefty, and these beefy tomatoes are looking good."* His dad and the rest of the family had not seen or had any contact with this lady for years. James was not certain of the relationship between the family and Ms. K. His dad pulled James to the back of the group and stated that Ms. K looked the same now as she did when he was a small boy. *'It must have been the country life and her mean looking demeanour, which kept her preserved and frozen in time,' thought* James.

The next thing Ms. K remarked was, "When did you arrive in town"*?* She did not even ask, how was the family or even said good morning. Imagine if they in-turn had ignored her when they entered the market that day? James's side of the family would have been the gossip of the entire marketplace or at the Town Hall monthly bash.

Instead, James took it on himself to say, "*We just arrived in town."*

She in turn said, "*That is not what I asked."*

Then James replied, "*A few days ago."*

She said, "*And it is only today you came to see me?* You are all not staying with family. When are you leaving? You-all too high and mighty to stay with family? Something wrong with the family who helped you get your business started?"

They had to get out of the market fast. James remained calm and waved to her after their purchases of two pounds of strawberries and grapes: only to hear her say, "*Well, what did you all bring for me?*" They shook their heads and moved on without responding.

The next stop the family visited on the way was Mr. Stern. Driving up the road the local news broadcasted loudly from the door which was open.

Dad yelled out, "*Mr. Stern, are you there?*" As they stepped inside the door , there was Mister S sitting by the window. His window faced the path, so he did see them coming, and did not say a word when they called his name. *Stubborn old man he was.*

James said, "*Good afternoon Mr. Stern.* What is going on with you?" *The Marvin Gaye's song (**What's Going On**)* wanted to burst from James' lips after he said that to the older man.

Mr. Stern would not have been too keen if James had begun singing the song. He kept a civil look on his face, but still thinking of the song he did not speak or utter another word.

James' dad spoke up firmly saying, "*The family came a day ago and wanted to visit and find out if you received any of the letters my wife wrote to you. She was concerned about your wellbeing and did not know whether or not you moved or went to live with your children.*" (No mentioning if he had passed on.)

Mr. Stern found his voice and spoke: "*This is the house my parents built, I was born here, and raised twelve kids here. Why ask such a stupid question? You would think that people with your fancy education know better.*"

"*Why did you not respond to the letters?*" Mother asked Mr. Stern.

He just said, "*Do you not see my hands are arthritic?*" Mr. Stern, clamped his lips together and swung his feet around his chair and turned his back the family.

Dad asked him if he needed anything more before the family was to return home.

Without turning around his answer were the exact words that Ms. Know-it-all spoke earlier "*Well, what did you all bring for me?*" James searched his memory and thought, 'What was it with the older folks saying the same thing when relatives or guests visited?'

The family chorused their farewell to the back of Mr. Stern's figure and exited his home.

"Two elders down and more to visit," Mother voiced. Up a beaten path the James and the family climbed to see Ms. No-zey. She was on her veranda doing her crochet.

"Hello there," Dad shouted out to her. Mother said, "*We are the Bonding family from up North.*" Ms. No-zey brisked and said, "*I know the family, and I am not blind. You came to see if I was alive? Well, what did you bring for me?*" (There were those famous spoken words again.)

Mother spoke clearly: *"This is a basket of food and some clothes for you."* Ms. No-zey piped up, "*Do I look like I am sick or not able to look after myself? I did not ask for handouts.*"

James, whispered to his mother, "*The family did not come all this way to get insulted or ridiculed by someone who is not even close family. She was so ungrateful.*"

Dad should have said to her, *'You take what we bring and go about your life.'*

Instead, Father quickly spoke to Ms. N saying sweetly, "*What was brought for you were items we thought you would make use of.*"

To top it off, she had the nerve to say, "*Do you know what, I could use some extra bars of soap, and Hats for church and flour to bake my cakes to sell.*"

Mom and Dad quickly rushed to say their goodbyes, when she proclaimed, *"You are all leaving in two weeks; do you think one of you can stop by and bring the things I just talked about? No need to go out of your way for me. If you can afford to come for holiday you all can spare those things. I hope that you could bring the items next week."*

She really gave us the thick and heavy guilt trip that weighed us down.

Realization blossomed in James' mind to show just how well the older men and women managed to survive for so long, if they do not have relatives to help them. The sly and crafty ways of the older Folks permeate deeply into the minds of anyone who happens to visit or a family member who frequently visit them on occasion.

This guilt has a BAIT, a HOOK, and a LINE. They reel you in like a fish or lure you into their webs as a spider does. Once you are in the older folk's vicinity, your minds are subliminally overtaken, and there is no escaping their tentacles. Unless you had the strength to stay away from them with a clear conscience.

The Older Folks Will Remain Set in Their Ways unless We too Change How We Treat Them.

WHY? WHY NOT

He: Come with me. Let us go away together: you and me, Now!

She: Now? Did you just say Now? Where are we going?

He: Just the two of us, somewhere.

She: Do you have a plan? Is it for the weekend?

To myself: *'Is he out of his M I N D?'*

He: Just say yes. We can stay for as long as you want.

She: This is not an engagement trick is it? If I say yes, will you tell me where this place is? Can I change my mind if I do not like the choice?

To myself. *'Should I commit without hearing where he is going or when he will return?'*

He: NO. You cannot change your mind. Your word seals the deal.

She: I need more details. How are we getting to this place? Tell me where we are going?

To myself. *'Who does he think he is? I will not be blinded into something I do not know about.'*

He: Since you cannot say YES, then I will not tell you where.

She: Saying YES now will be disastrous. I need time to think clearly about this sudden invitation. I have my job to think about. I have to put in a request to take the time off.

To myself. *'Does he think I am going to fall for that trick?'*.

He: All you have to say is, YES, you will go with me. Nothing you have to pack. Everything I will buy for you.

She: Is this a secluded getaway? Are we staying in the city? Are we going out of town? Do I need to take time off from work?

To myself. *'Is he in trouble? What did he do? Should I be scared?*

He: What is your answer?

She: NO.

He: How can you say NO so easily to something you do not know about?

She: I just did. NO.

He: I will go alone.

She: Alone? Hmmmm? Do enjoy your alone time. Have a wonderful getaway. So, tell me, where are you going?

He: I am not telling you where I am going. You could have said, Yes, and come away with me.

She: The answer is still No. So come on, tell me where will you be going?

He: I do not know.

She: You asked me to go with you and you do not know where you are going?

He: I know. I know. I had hoped you would say *Yes.* Then I would have decided on a special destination or allow you to choose.

She: That was your plan? You really mean to tell me that that was the plan you had in mind? You had no plan in the first place. You asked me to go away with you and there was never a plan? My answer is not changing.

He: Is your answer still, *No*?

She: YES!

He: Yes! you will go with me, or No, you will not go with me?

She: YES. The answer is still NO!

TIME TO GET UP

Morning! – Already?

The sun had not risen, and the Rooster was awake. Little Johnny was asleep when the Rooster began with the noise! Cock-a-doodle-doo. Cock-a-doodle-doo. Cock-a-doodle-doo.

"If he keeps on with that noise over and over he will be barbequed or chicken soup by the afternoon for sure." Little Johnny turned over in bed to snuggle some more.

Cock-a-doodle-doo. Cock-a-doodle-doo. Cock-a-doodle-doo. *That noisy Rooster* is making that noise again,.

" *What time is it anyway?*" Little Johnny felt on the side table for the old-fashioned clock. The time showed, "*Four in the morning? How does that Rooster do it each day?*"

No Clock!

No Alarm!

No Light!

Little Johnny gets out of bed, shuffles around, flips on the light and greets the day. Again, the Rooster doodled louder *as if he was under the bed.* Little Johnny forcefully slides open the window and peers into the dark morning and yells at the invisible Rooster, "*I'm up. I am up! I have awoken! Do you not hear me?*"

Time to start his summer internship. He did not have the luxury to lounge in the bunk or lay idle. This was his summer-in-the-country. His friends went on retreats or sleep away camps with other children. Not like this camp on the farm of Grand-Pa Knight.

Little Johnny wanted to fulfil his internship requirements. Prior to visiting the Knight's farm, he swore into secrecy with a strict no sharing about the grooming and racing techniques. Johnny was to tell no one of the animal feed that was in the horse's diet, or the training workouts for the horses, or the jockeys that would ride on race day. Little Johnny did not know what the strict codes had to do with been on a farm before he arrived. All that he wanted was to be at the racetrack to see the horse races: especially if it was the horses he helped to train. The thrill of watching the pounding hoofs galloping around the oval would not come until he had passed all of his Knight's test. The Knights Clan did not disclose to Johnny what the Knight's test was all about.

He worked every day to follow the strict rules and protocols and prepared the horses for the derby. Johnny would gallop the horses before the trainers arrived. He would massage the horses and give them the correct amount of grains and water. Too much feed would make the horses sluggish on race day. *He remembered that one rule at the beginning of his indoctrination into the Knights Clan.*

Every grandchild that arrived at the Knights' Summer Cottage of his grandparents had to intern for three months. The youngest of the grandchildren started the early shift, and Little Johnny would later learn it was the initiation sequence to becoming a True Knight.

The light was beginning to filter in: Dawn! He sipped his hot cocoa and munched down his hot buttered scones before he trotted to the barn for his daily routine. He could not wait to be older on his summer visits. The Older Knights resided in the Kings Club closer to the Town. *The roosters never cross the highway to wake up the knighted clan members.* The older Knights focused on training to be jockeys and mastering the financial side of the Horse Racing Business. They had fun by participating in the winner's circle festivities, playing rounds of golf, and sailing at the yacht clubs on the weekends. This was every Knights summer dream.

For being the youngest intern as a Farmhand, he prepared the young horses for their daily training. He cleaned out the stalls, fed the horses, groomed them, and helped with the preliminary training. Johnny had to know when to canter or trot the horses and when they needed speed workouts. Knowing the racing schedules of the horses and the mileage to train, required practice and patience. The horses had mandatory early morning gallops to avoid the heat later in the day. That would account for the early rooster rising of Little Johnny-Knight.

Each animal needs were different. Little Johnny learned in his initiation that each horse required a different type of feed depending on the distances the horses raced. *'When did animals get a menu list to choose from?'* Little Johnny's mind churned with knowledge as he worked through his internship.

The sun and Johnny were in a constant race. Day in, Day out. *No rest for the weary intern.* Little Johnny would begin the cycle all over again before sunset.

Up, Down.

Down, Up.

So much to do and not enough time for fun. He was not complaining, but he wanted to engage in fun time now and again. He tried to hurry through is morning phases of the internship: yet he was very thorough. Lunch break was only one hour, but he wanted to spend it by fishing or bowling with Grand-Pa Knight. That was his fun time which was not long enough.

Little Johnny Knight had to perform his tasks with precision and maintain the Knight standards.

Why? At any given time, a higher-ranking Knight would present his or herself unannounced. Little Johnny observed them with sideways glances as they recorded their notes and inspected his daily work. None of the interns knew what time of the day the inspectors would arrive to oversee his tasks.

During the day, the horses needed more rub downs after their intensive training. Sometimes Little Johnny watched and observed the workers either with training or tending to the horses before he felt comfortable replicating the methods himself.

In the afternoons, he hastened back to his internship, to coral the horses back to the barn, replenish the stalls with clean hay, and give the animals fresh water and new feed.

Even when it rained, and no sun visible, the Rooster who awaked like MILITARY Clock Work, interrupted Little Johnny's sleep, with the signature – Cock-a-doodle-doo: Cock-a-doodle-doo: Cock-a-doodle-doo.

Johnny learned in life, in order to win your **Prize, you must be Early to Rise and exceptionally Wise.**

DID IT EXIST?

Re-visiting life in Paradise.

To you, it was a perfect place, this island called Le Blanchet.

A dream of all dreams place.

Paradise existed on Le Blanchet for you.

To find out if it did exist, let us travel back.

What did you expect to see?

Did you hope to see Le Blanchet as it was 50 years ago?

Would your Paradise recognize you or would you recognize Paradise?

You imagined that you could rewind the past and expect things to be as it was when you left Le Blanchet half a century ago. Will you see where you once lived looking as it did when you left long ago?

Or will you look back as LOT's wife did while fleeing from where she had lived? Look what happened to her? Frozen in time!

Live now.

Live in the present.

It is a GIFT!

Embrace what is here.

What prevailed long ago, cannot exist today.

Who can narrate the story from your point of view? Only you can do that.

Wanting to revisit your Paradise in Le Blanchet after being away, you hoped it was the same place as when you left.

You are older: The surroundings have altered to reflect the progression of time. **It is modernization**.

The friends you once knew have ventured on. **It is migration.**

You meet new people. Old relationships have vanished. They have moved in a different direction. You become disoriented, trying to see the past while existing in the present. Nothing is recognizable. It has changed. **It is progression.**

Where is it? This **Paradise?**

You are the only one to bring to life in details the events as it was long ago. The way the days made you feel inside. Happy, mischievous, adventurous, carefree, or disappointed. The tension on that one day when you dashed out to view the Ceremonial launching of the ship. It was a nautical tradition seen by the town. The blessing of the ship was a grand celebration.

You can recall vividly the wind blowing and caressing your face as the smell of the ocean tickled your nostrils when you awaited the noise of the champagne bottle smashing across the bow of the new ship.

You recall the sounds of the huge sails that flapped in the breeze as the ship strained on the ropes wanting to be free. Excitement circulated within as you enthusiastically hopped around in the sand as if it were too hot. Everyone around you were patiently waiting to hear the NAMING of the ship as the ropes released and the ship launched forward into the rhythmic ocean waves.

What a moment that was for you. You: watching the ship roll across the logs and hearing the sounds of the splash when the ship entered the water. The bobbing of the ship as the water met the oak wood and the waves lashing about the sides, was enough to bring tears of joy streaming down your face.

Who else can conjure up what you saw, or how you felt that day? Each individuals' moments are unique and special. Are you familiar with the phrase – (seeing is believing). There is truth in that phrase, and in the minds of those who lived it. One yearns to transport back to see the life that helped shape them into who they are now. Individuals crave to venture back to fix the past to right the wrong or take something from the past to be superior in the future. Little do they realize that by changing the past the future may not exist. Holding onto the past can stifle them from progressing in the present. Their outcomes could be the opposite of what they had hoped.

You thought to see the **Paradise** in where you lived years ago!

If you do not see the evidence of what you knew: Did it exist?

If only you could reproduce a visual proof of Paradise to make seeing it now more tangible!

The evidence or proof of its existence is in your
Memory Chip of a Mind.

THE FEUD

I am talking to you. Yes, you, and you, too. Do not look around and say to yourself, she is not talking to me. She cannot be talking to me. It is you, to whom I am talking.

Yes: I am talking to You and You and to all of you. Especially, you.

Holiday time! Have you ever heard of a Vacation!

If not now, then when? Time to get away to the warm climate and clean beaches. If not there: then a quiet lakeside country retreat. It is time for you to get away, leave all the hectic work and responsibilities to someone else. Wake up on an island in an all-inclusive hotel. Activities for the kids to enjoy and you; yes you, can relax and unwind.

Who would not want this thing called Vacation for a week?

You deserve the break.

You worked hard.

You saved up.

You need this Vacation, and you will enjoy this Vacation.

A DEDICATION TO YOU – THE TOURIST

Whether the getaway is close to home or on an Exotic island, YOU WANT SUN all day and night if possible. You want a Sun-Tan. Yes a Suntan. Every day you want to head to a pool or a beach and bronze your physique.

Why? When you return home after your vacation, you want to hear your friends say to you, "*You look younger. You look well rested. Nice tan!*"

You do not want to see a drop of rain on your week's stay. The only water you want to see is the one in the SEA or in the POOL or what you DRINK. The holiday is Rain Free to Tan Thee. You did not come all this way to pay for rain. The rain will not be an extra addition to your All-Inclusive trip. You want what you paid for. Rain Not Included.

NOW, DEDICATED TO YOU – THE NATIVES

Going home to reconnect or to spend time with the family. Are you fed up and tired of the umbrellas, the wet days, the cold, the snow, the crowds, and the fast pace? It is time for beach and quiet. The only water you need is the one you drink from the coconut tree.

How about daily sun's rays to warm your skin and to elevate your mood? Or a view of the Ocean from your hotel window instead of an all too familiar place? The sound of the waves making their way to your ears. Not the sounds of car horns or sirens blasting in your ears. The sounds of chirping exotic birds as they flutter by to drink nectar from the flowers is what you want to hear and see.

A break from Sky Juice falling on you. Rain is not on the menu. The only thing on your menu is a festival and a cook-out. All this joy and relaxation could bring you the peace of mind you have been longing for.

BREAKING NEWS FLASH!

The Exotic Island is experiencing a drought. **Drought**?

The locals are praying for Rain. They claim the land and the soil is dry and parched. The place is looking more brown than green. The water levels in the reservoirs are way below the normal range. The plump fruits are half the size. It is not as if the tourist will notice. All they come to do is Tan, Tan, Tan. We locals want the rain, rain, rain, to pour, pour, and pour.

The animals are lean. The government regulated that lean meat is the new trending health craze. However, having Prime Ribs listed on the menu will look like Bone Ribs. The T-Bone steak on your plate will look like a **T,** with Bone, with a hint of meat.

No rainfall for weeks. This is when you will on see vast areas of dry grass on the sides of the road, on the golf courses, and in the yards in front of our homes.

Dry grass with hot sun causes bush fires. Is that what you want for us?

Dry grass is not the best for the cows to eat. The cows chew green, so brown grass is not pristine.

Prime cows are plump but lean on the rump.

YOU TOURIST: who are wishing for SUN?

How did you get so much power over the RAIN?

Tourist, we locals need rain for our produce to sell in the market. How can you expect us to get good $$$$ for half nourished vegetables? The potatoes look like peanuts and the bananas look like string beans.

Come on people. Let the Rain Fall. You do not even want it to rain at night. Why? You want to party all night. Give us a break. Can you not give us the night rain? You had your Day Tan.

Please, let us compromise. **Let the Water** – REIGN **and let the Sun** – BEAM. *That seems like a fair enough deal. Let us work as a* TEAM.

THE LOST ONES

Do you remember the Nursery Rhyme, *Little Bo Peep who lost her sheep!* Nathan and his two brothers had their lost lambs one day. Little children attended sheep and goats in the country-side as they went to school and matured. It was the typical way of life. Children took the animals to pasture and allowed them to graze early in the morning and collected them just before sundown.

Knowing how to guide the sheep and goats up the mountain side or down the paths was not a taught skill. Skills became perfected and ingrained as they cared for the animals. It was as if the youths mastered their trade as they worked and applied common sense to keep the animals together.

Nathan the leader at twelve, knew how to tether the goats and sheep in such a place that they did not escape or become tangled. When the animals become tangled they become stressed and struggled on their ropes which leads to trauma. To avoid the animals becoming tangled Nathan was attentive to the surroundings.

Parents did not give children stakes at a young age to loop the ropes and secure their herd. The siblings found sections in the grass to tether the animals when no trees were near. Specials ways to select the right grass stumps and use the ropes to tie their livelihood was vital. The three siblings did what was necessary to graze their animals safely in the pastures early in the mornings. The lambs were always free to frolic they were never too far from their mothers. After leaving the pasture, Nathan and his brothers returned home and headed off to their sailing lessons.

The Captain was expecting them at the sailing dock eight o'clock sharp. The brothers were excited to have the instructor Captain Topper as their teacher. He was the most honoured and respected Sailor in town. Today was the first day for the sailing lessons. Nathan joined the sailing group for one special reason. He wanted to be the Captain of his own boat one day.

Captain Topper instructed the brothers about the lifeboats and the location of the safety hatches. Before any sailing, the Captain instructed the children about water safety. The brothers were avid swimmers. Nathan was an adapt learner and listened intently to Captain Topper's instructions on the terminology of rope tying. Type of knots and tying techniques that Nathan learned were the *Square Knots, The Bowline, and The Sailors Hitch.*

Nathan attended his daily lessons in preparation for the Regatta Festival. The number of races at a regatta is equal to the number of teams competing times two divisions. The youths' races only composed of four teams with eight races competing simultaneously. Nathan and his brothers were part of the youth team competition.

After the sailing lessons, the brothers and Nathan returned to the pasture to retrieve the animals. Picture the brother's horror upon arriving at the pasture for their flock. Nathan noticed his perfect rope tying knots undone from the mother sheep rope. The mother's feet tangled with the ropes around a huge boulder. The mother sheep had no lambs around her. She was bleating non-stop loudly and very skittish when Nathan tried to unravel her from the ordeal. The younger brothers panicked! Nathan was skilled and knew how to fasten and tie knots, so he was confused by the scene he and his brothers were witnessing.

He was the eldest.

He was the individual they all looked up to.

They all looked around frantically in the grassy pasture, but no lambs were in sight. Going home without the lambs was not an option for the trio. The brothers searched one way and Nathan searched in the other direction in vain as the sun was setting. Neighbouring children were rounding up their flocks and guiding them to their homes.

Nathan asked a rival neighbour who had his flock gathered, for help. The neighbour did not offer any aid. With no sounds heard by the lambs in the area, the brothers and Nathan crossed the road hoping to seek out little lambs.

Sometimes, sheep wandered away in search of tastier grass when the surrounding grass was not as lush. He prayed they would find the lambs soon. He had nothing to lose by going across the road even though lambs do not wander far from their mother. Nathan thought to himself, 'Were the lambs playing hide and seek. It was not a good time to be hiding.' It was a grassier and greener on the property that Mr. Johnson owned across the road. A construction phase was in progress on the land.

The two younger brothers grabbed Nathan's hands and sobbed, "What are we going to do if we do not find the lambs?" Nathan was also scared about the same thing, but he did not show that fear on his face. He comforted his brothers by squeezing their shoulders and marched forward.

As the group neared a foundation on the other side of the hill, they increased their pace upon hearing soft bleating sounds with no sighting of the lambs.

"Where were those sound coming from?" One of his brothers voice shakily said. "It is impossible for snow white lambs to blend in with the green grass."

Nathan heard the bleating louder as he was the climbing up a small incline in a secluded area. His brothers hurried pass him and neared to the sounds from the lost lambs were coming from under a wooden plank on the ground.

"*Why would the lambs be under there?*" Nathan spoke angrily.

The brothers managed to slide the plank back to see the lambs in the shallow hole resembling a pit. One brother jumped in and hoisted the lambs out one at a time.

Andrew the youngest brother spoke up by saying, "There was no way the lambs would hide under a wooden plank by themselves. They do not know anything about hide and go seek."

"Someone did want to swindle the lambs indeed," Nathan said in a relieved happy tone of voice.

Shepherd's Pie? Shish Kabob? Curried Lamb? Hmmmm!

It was much later than usual for them to be heading home. Darkness was nearing and no streetlights to brighten up the path home.

Therefore, the bothers rushed hastily back across the road holding the lambs to see the rest of the flock bleating loudly and nervously waiting. The lambs mother especially sounded the loudest hearing her lost babies whimpering bleats.

Thank goodness the white lambs were safe before someone had **Slaughtered** and **Stewed** them for Sunday Dinner. Nathan, less anxious, and comforted knowing that he followed his instincts by searching for the lambs on the other side of the road. He also realized that the lessons at the Sailing class would be beneficial. Learning to use diverse types of knots were important for the boat's safety. The knots secured the sails and anchored the boats. As a result, the safety knot tying lessons would help the brothers in keeping their sheep and goats securely tied when they carried them to pasture.

Lessons learned at a new task can be beneficial in the improvement of old skills.

EYE OPENER

The two sisters journeyed to Italy with no directives, no preparation, and no clue of what to expect of them in the foreign place. Do you want to know what they saw when they arrived in Italy? It was not the Leaning Tower of Pisa nor the Colosseum.

Upon exiting the airport, both girls witnessed flashing lights as though it was the Pontiff Motor Cage racing to the Cathedral. The loud noises bleared from sirens on huge white trucks roaring down the motor way. They witnessed cars switching back and forth in and out of lanes as if jockeying for positions on a racetrack and thought it was chaos. Petrified, both girls hid in their seats and covered their ears.

Tracey and Heather had been enjoying their daily lives on the tiny Isla-de-Espano. Both girls ate at the family restaurant every day, listened to popular music played at the Inn, and socialized with celebrities who visited the Happy-Eats Restaurant.

The girls helped out at the Eat-Inn Restaurant as the place was friendly called. During the week they shadowed the older girls by overseeing things in the kitchen or maintained and organized the Eat-Inn's decorum. The silver ware and plates for the guests strategically placed correctly. Maintaining and keeping the dining areas spotless, along with taking the customers' orders were a part of the customs.

The boy's contributions to the family business involved providing fresh cuisine for the daily menu. The men went fishing for Calamari or shrimp or the catch of day and the boys went along to learn the trade. Learning meant knowing where it was best to fish (depending on the weather), making sturdy Lobsters traps, and cleaning the fish when they returned to shore.

Daily bustling and constant customers at the Happy-Eats Restaurant were good for business. The younger girls seating the clients at the tables allowed the older ladies to focus on the cooking or bringing the meals to the guests quickly: along with placing orders to carry-out.

The customers gathered on Thursdays for a variety of Pizza Dishes, Fridays for Fish of the day or Brodetto-Soup and Saturday afternoons for Spaghetti alle Vongole. Singing and Dancing was the norm for the lively place. The three days at the end of the week were the busiest. Tuesdays and Wednesdays were reservation days for guest. Booking early was essential. Wednesdays included entertaining bands for the musical night. The sisters knew the latest songs and artists because they heard them first-hand at the restaurant.

On Isla-de-Espano, the Eat-Inn was Tracey and Heather's main home with a traditional family atmosphere. One day the girl's older cousin informed them of a visitor coming from overseas.

'Was there such a place Over the Seas? Where was this place? Was this visitor coming from the other side of the island?'

The next day the family piled into the car and drove to the airport. Imagine six people travelling to the airport to great one person! Tracey and Heather were too excited to understand that it made no sense.

Arriving at the airport, the family watched the Uncle through the fence as he deplaned. The entire family waved and bounced up and down as he came through the door. The family group hugged, and the Uncle spoke softly saying, "*I want to sleep.*"

SLEEP Tracey thought? *'It was early in the morning. He should be wide awake.'* He was their distant Uncle Giovanni.

It was not until later the two girls found out that he travelled from Italy. The morning after, while the Uncle was up and about, he ate breakfast at the Eat-Inn. Tracey and Heather kept their distance because Uncle-Gio and the older family members conversed constantly. Anytime Tracey tried talking with Uncle-Gio, their cousin would intervene by telling her to take the meal orders to the kitchen for the customers. The family establishment had to maintain their ambitious standards of speedy service. Tracey wanted her family business to prosper, so she obeyed and did not annoy her uncle.

It turned out that Uncle-Gio was a popular man. People would show up when he was sitting under the Gazebo facing the water and addressed him as Caro Padre. They shook his hands and Uncle-Gio seemed to bless them. Heather wondered if he was a priest. He did not look like a priest: but he was attentive when they spoke to him. Heather observed the visitors bobbing their heads up and down when Uncle-G spoke back to them. After they conversed with her uncle for a while, he would give them something.

"It had to be money," Heather said to Tracey after spying on the encounters. The visitors left with a smile of relief on their faces and walked as though they floated on air.

The Uncle stayed two weeks on Isla-de-Espano, before returning to Italy. Later in the day before their uncle left, he whispered to Heather and Tracey that they should come to visit him in Italy.

Three years later both girls were on their way to Italy. "It is *time to find out where this Uncle lived,*" Heather informed Tracey.

Little did they know that their trip was more than just a visit to their Uncle-Gio.

The franchise of the Happy-Eats Restaurant needed internal updates and improvements on the building decor. That was how the family envisioned what was necessary to revamp the Restaurant business. In order for the new changes and improvements to take place, innovative solutions and education in technology would benefit the Family Business.

Technology included the latest computers was the upcoming trend coming to the Eat-Inn to help business to flourish and reach more customers and to broaden the Food Catering outreach. The technology with the latest programs, would calculate and manage the profits and wage transactions much faster. This would reduce the time spent on tallying the books with pen and paper.

Who better to learn and bring new skills back to Isla-de-Espano, than the *Two young ladies, Heather, and Tracey*? The technology was something the young girls should master and eventually teach the younger and older ladies.

The family heard of other restaurants managers talking about the influx of tourism. The Eat-Inn take-out Pizza menus needed to include variety of new toppings due to the diversity in clientele.

The restaurant family members reminded the girls before they left:

- *Learn all that there is to learn.*
- *Do not be rude.*
- *Do not go certain places alone.*
- *Do not talk to strangers.*

Tracey pondered! *'What can both of them do if they are told* ***Do not do this or do not do that****'?*

That was the extent to the instructions, speech, and guidance the girls received. They whispered to each other and shared how scared they felt. Tracey shared; "*This Italian trip did not sound so fun after the (Do Not's) that was said. Staying on* Isla-de-Espano, *would be better.*"

The entire family travelled with the two girls to the airport. Arriving at the airport the girls realized that no one had prepared them for the transition they were about to embark upon. Both girls boarded the airplane that would change their future.

After hours and hours in the air, they had arrived.

Benvenuto in Italia – Welcome to Italy was said over the loud-speaker as the girls exited the airplane.

Both girls felt *COLD while they waited for the luggage to reach them.* Heather said to Tracey: "*They were busy telling us what not to do, they forgot to educate us on what to expect. Certainly, they never went to Italy.*"

Tracey replied, "Adults *think they know it all because they are older than us. Deep down, they really do not know anything.*"

The girls collected their luggage and cleared them with the immigration officers. As they nervously walked towards the exit the girls' heard chants of their names. They scanned the faces to see Uncle-Gio who had told them to come to visit him. He was not at the airport to meet them. Only the new faces waving and calling their names. As they got closer to the group, one of them yelled,

"Uncle Gio said to meet you both."

Heather inquired, "Where was he?"

No one answered Heather's question as a relative helped the girls with their luggage to the transport. The family and both girls slipped into a Mini Van and were off to see the new place. The minivan sped along the multi-lane highway as if the paparazzi were chasing them.

Tracey thought, "Was that the reason for the flashing lights behind the van as they drove faster and faster?"

Heather was not expecting to see buildings higher than two stories in height.

"Where are the little homes." Heather muttered to Tracey? *"Why are the buildings so tall?"*

The Mini Van screeched to a halt in front of an apartment building. When the girls exited the van a series of glass doors, affronted them. Never had they seen so many glass doors.

"*Where is the furniture,*" Tracey exclaimed?

They looked at each other wide eyed. Eventually they passed through a passage and then to a door which a cousin opened. The apartment was located along the passageway. Entering the apartment, the vision the girls came upon was not familiar.

Their cousin served them supper and advised them to get to bed and rest. The next day was a school day.

"What! School? You must be kidding. I thought we came to see our Uncle," Tracey said aloud to the cousin.

"We just arrived! No sightseeing? No getting to know the place."

"I am too tired and confused to think," said Tracey.

Both sisters went to bed and awoke the next day to see their Cousin Queeny. "When did she arrive," Tracey declared to Heather when Cousin-Q left the room? Cousin Queeny had left the island before the girls, but Heather and Tracey were not aware she was in Italy.

They looked at each other and shrugged. Cousin Queeny advised the girls to eat their breakfast and get themselves ready to leave the apartment.

It was **Training Day**.

The girls threw on their jackets and gloves and told to follow Cousin-Q. Gloves! Both girls wondered why? Stepping outside, they felt the chill and were incredibly grateful for the gloves. Cousin-Q and the girls walked for 5 minutes to the train depot. A loud racket sounded as the girls looked around to see where the noise was coming from. Cousin-Q hauled them back from the edge of the platform. Shaken up, they both looked peeved at their cousin, but did not speak. Shocked at Cousin-Q for jerking them backwards and watching the long speedy train roar into the station.

Tracey could not share her thoughts aloud with Heather due to the noisy racket and their cousin dragging them into the train when the doors opened.

Packed crowds of people like sardines squeezed around the ladies while a voice echoed, **'Le Porte di chiusura per favore' – *'Watch the closing doors please.'*** Both girls stared at the doors mesmerized and looking around wondering who said those words.

With no place to move while standing in the train, Cousin-Q pointed to a pole and grabbed their hands around the pole. Both held on for dear life as the noisy train raced at top speed along the rails. Suddenly they heard, "**Prossima fermata, Napoli." "Next stop Naples."** Cousin-Q motioned towards the open doors and pulled the girls off the train. As they departed the train and walked upstairs and outside, the crowds pushed them along.

Heather mumbled, *"We did not get any input on what was going to happen today or to where we were to go."*

Tracey said, *"This must be the new way things are done in Italy."*

Cousin-Q – guided the two perplexed girls into a building on the other side of Piazza Mancini. Asking them to sit on the chairs while she conversed with the Gentleman in Italian at the front desk. The Gentleman and their cousin spoke for a while and then he motioned them to come forward.

He introduced himself to them as Mr. Ponoso. "*Benvenoto, Alunna.*" *Welcome to* The School of Catering and Technology, *please follow me.* Tracey and Heather gaped at each other and in unison said, "*Good Morning Mr. Ponoso.*"

They immediately looked around to ask questions of their Cousin-Q. However, she was nowhere in sight.

Both girls blindly followed Mr. *Ponoso* to a hall with rows and rows of girls seated at long tables. He motioned for Heather to sit on one side and Tracey on the opposite side. They faced each other.

In the center of the tables were stacks of cutlery, bowls, plates, glasses, and cloth napkins. In the front of the room was an enormous screen. A gentleman stood to the left of the podium speaking into a microphone mouthing, "Silenzioso, Silenzioso, Silenzioso, Tutti" – "Quiet-Quiet-Quiet everyone."

"Today is the first of your **Training Day Ladies**. You are here to be waiters and hosts extraordinaire. You will be learning how to use the computers and tablets to increase work productivity. Let the journey begin towards your successful careers into the restaurant business. Be ready to face the world as the world needs you to face it to make a change."

Tracey looked across at Heather and mouthed, ***Welcome to a New World – The Italian Connection.***

PAIN IN THE ELDER

Nothing had prepared Louise for the multiple events that would transpire in the next few weeks to come. She had one agenda in mind but someone else had a hidden one for her. Little did she know what was coming her until it was too late. Honourable deeds when done without a purpose creates unusual endings any day.

Leisurely strolling down to the beach as she did each day at dawn, Louise stretched before she swam her daily laps in the ocean. As she meandered to the water she passed an older man (AKA The Elder – Mr. E) sitting in the sand massaging his knees.

When she passed she politely said, "*Good morning sir, How are you today?*"

The Elder replied, "My knees are aching; I am going to get into the water to ease the pain. I have back pains, I have sugar diabetes, and high blood pressure. I should visit the doctor to get new prescriptions because the old ones are not working."

Louise spoke and said, "*I hear the sea water helps with the pains.*"

The Elder, "You know I went yesterday but the special doctor who I usually speak too was not there. I am not sure when he will come back. I do not like the one that was there yesterday, but I need my prescriptions."

Louise suggested, "Why not go back tomorrow and check if the doctor you want to speak to is in the office."

The Elder, "They tell me that as you get older, the back aches, and the joints aches. Today I will visit a doctor for my knee pain and another doctor for my back pain. One Doctor should do all the work. That would stop my multiple visits to the doctor's office."

Louise responded, "I hope you will be able to see someone that you want." "I should get my laps in before the sun gets too hot."

She swam her laps for a while and got out of the water, only to see the Elder getting into the water.

The older man approached Louise. "**Not again,**" Louise grunted under her breath.

As if he thought Louise was deaf, he shouted out, "I hope my knees do not pain so much for my trip. I am travelling in two weeks; I need my pills."

She responded, "*Ok, Mr. E,"* and quickly hurried to wash the salt off from her skin before heading back home.

The following day, Louise arrived at the beach to swim. She walked to a shallow spot to enter the water when she noticed something in the sand. It was Mr. E, buried in the sand up to his neck. Of course, she extends the polite form of respect.

The Elder began his speech: "I was told the sand is good for joint pains. I must get to the doctor today for my pills to ease the pain in my joints and to keep my pressure lower."

Louise was *trying to sneak away politely,* but before she did leave , she remarked, "Did you not visit the doctor yesterday after you left the beach?"

The Elder, "The doctor was not there. Maybe I should go back today."

Louise hurriedly replied, "Ok. I am leaving now."

This routine seemed to go on day after day. Louise switched the time she arrived at the beach and where she entered. *'No elder in sight,' she chuckled to herself.*

Guess who was approaching to her amazement on her final lap one exceedingly early morning?

It must have been Louise's red hair that gave Mr. E clear sighting of her while she was in the water.

Louise acknowledged the elder and inquired about his well-being as well as referring to his joint pains.

The Elder sweetly asked her, "*Are you leaving already?* I came in to take a sea bath to help sooth my aching joint. I am going to the doctors to see what they can do for my arthritis."

Louise sighed, and said, "Mr. *E, I have been in the water for a while, and I must go home. Sorry or not having the time to chat with you today."*

She had to think about going to another beach that was not too far or out of the way. She left as fast as she could and was happy that she had arrived earlier than usual.

The next week Louise signed up for a Boat trip to Guadeloupe. The Ferry was leaving at four o'clock sharp in the morning. The tour agent requested that passengers use Euros for payment towards the selected tours before the day of departure.

The Agent was not certain if the exchange banks or Cambio's would be available once they disembarked in the foreign country. Therefore, Louise rushed quickly to get her exchange currency for the tours. When she walked into the bank, a huge NO MORE EUROS flashed in front of her on a sign. The teller acknowledged that none of the other banks had Euros either.

Louise hurried back to the Tour office to talk with the tour guide to ask if she could pay for her tours before she left, in Australian Currency. She Agent said, "NO! NO!"

"Why," Louise retorted?

The Agent said, "*It had to be in Euros.*"

Devastated but not feeling down, she was not giving up on her quest to find a way to pay for the tour exertions to Guadeloupe.

'Hopefully the Cambio in the Mall was open when they arrived at their destination,' Louise thought to herself.

She arrived at the Ferry Port early. No one was recognizable to her while she waited at Two-Thirty in the morning at the jetty with the other travellers. She prayed that luck was with her. When the Immigration documents and customs had concluded, the boarding onto the ferry had commenced for the group to leave on time.

It was four o'clock, and the Ferry remained docked. Four fifteen and still no movement. The passengers were getting restless by now. Louise looked out the porthole and saw someone hustling down the walkway.

'Whomever it was, they were sure late and moving fast.'

Just as she was about to relax, Louise heard a familiar voice as the passenger boarded, saying, "*Am I too late? I thought it was half-four o'clock departure?*"

'Oh No, Mr. E is going on the trip? He was never late when she went swimming each day.'

Louise could not believe the familiar sound in her ears. She bunkered down in the seat, tried to camouflage under her cardigan, and closed her eyes as the ferry pulled off.

Mr. E, must have been able to meet with his doctor for his prescriptions: which in turn helped him on that fast speed to reach the Ferry. Or was it because he was late?

Loud repetitions of, "**Ladies and Gentlemen we are in International Waters**," and bright lights brilliantly shone to awake the passengers when the ferry pulled close into the port of the foreign island. The tour guide addressed the passengers and informed them to remain seated until the Ferry docked for safety reasons. She continued to explain, "After docking, they should assemble around her when they disembarked and remain together until she had the tour groups parties sorted out."

The passengers departed the ferry and assembled next to the guide while Louise looked around for a Cambio to exchange her Australian $$$$ to Euros. The Cambio's that were located in the Port Authority were not open. The Huge Sign posted on the Bulletin Board in the immigration lobby read – 'Ce magasin est fermé' – 'Stores closed until 12 noon'.

'That meant no Euros for the tour,' thought Louise, who was frustrated and agitated. *'All this way and nothing to do for 9 hours if she could not exchange her $$$$ into Euros for the tours!'*

A brilliant Idea flashed instantly! She could ask one of the passengers to exchange her $$$$ for Euros. On second thought: who would want her Australian dollars? That idea she discarded from her mind.

Meanwhile, in the Taxi vestibule the tour guide announced: "Tour One – Plantation – Bus Number 1."

Passenger's hands went up waving the Euros. They boarded a Green Van, and off they went.

"Tour number Two – Waterfalls – Bus Number 2."

Similar scenarios as in tour One and Two continued to go on as the crowd dwindled. Hands raised and Euros waved when the tour guide said, "Rum Factory." A popular tour!

The designated tour buses filled up and off they went. There was a second bus and third bus for extra passengers to the favourite Rum Factory. Other tours went to the Water-Falls, the Historical Fort, and the Botanical Gardens.

Louise watched as each bus filled up with her compatriots and departed on their tours. The number of passengers were down to seven people remaining which included Louise, a lady and the Elder.

The Elder was fussing and complaining that he wanted to be on a tour.

The guide suggested, "*Plantation Tour?*"

The Elder replied, "Not that one."

She then suggested the "*Botanical Tour,*"

To that choice, again the Elder said, "No."

She asked questioned, "*Where do you want to go?*"

His response, "*The Plantation.*"

She seemed peeved at that point and retorted, "*When I asked you about that tour, you did not want to go. Well, where do you want to go now?*"

He echoed, "I do not know."

While the Elder was undecided, the Agent was able to get a small taxi for the other four passengers who had paid for a Historical Fort Tour. The group had been too large for the previous Bus. The guide conversed by a Taxi, with a man who was reading a paper and did not seem concerned about the remainder three passengers.

Quickly acknowledging the passenger that remained with Louise and was standing alone, Louise called out to the Lady and asked, "What tour did you sign up to explore?"

The lady's expression resembled a mime: A blank look – looking back at her.

Louise turned around and questioned the Elder about what he had planned to do when he arrived.

The elder said, *"He wanted to see Guadeloupe because he had never been out of the country."*

Louise then asked, "What about the Lady, do you know her?"

The Elder shrugged.

Louise, fed up with the Elder, baffled with the silent Lady, tense about having no euros tried something new, paced back and forth silently. She had to get through to the Lady because talking to the Elder was useless.

Again, she asked, "What tours did you sign up for before leaving?" With no response, she changed the question by saying, "When *you did not speak at first, were you shy?"* Still, the lady said nothing. In turn, Louise questioned the Elder, "*What was the issue with the lady?*"

Louise immediately realized that the Guide was about to get into a Taxi. She promptly dashed over to her to figure out something for their dilemma.

The Guide motioned to the Taxi to wait as she approached Mr. E and the lady.

She verbally said that no more tour taxis were available, the other taxis were off duty and waiting for the next Ferry to arrive.

The Elder piped in and said, "*I have Euros.*" The Guide placed her hands up in the air and began walking away.

Louise saw the day falling apart. In a quandy, she had to think swiftly or else they would stay in one spot for nine hours. Nothing to do, no place to go, and no one with whom they were familiar.

She hastily suggested, "What if the three took a taxi and ride around to sightsee?"

"Could the guide inquire from one of the off-duty taxi-men if that option was a possibility?" Not knowing the dialect, Louise was relying on the Guide to relay the correct message to the taxi man.

The Guide returned to group of three and said that a taxi-man agreed to do a semi tour to places the tourist do not frequent but were good sights. Louise queried the price: it was *70 Euros for four hours.*

Louise asked, "*Was it 70 Euros each?*"

The guide replied that it was for the three of them.

Louise was amazed the price was much lower than the individual fares for the tours the groups had left to explore earlier.

She hurried over and told the Elder what the Guide had arranged and said that it would be good for the three of them. The Elder mumbled, "I guess so. I suppose so. It has to do. We have to do something."

Then he spoke up and asked, "Where is the tour taking us? To the Market? To the Rum Factory?"

Louise, ignored him at this point. She was livid but did not show it. Louise took a deep breath and politely uttered, "The taxi man had to finish eating. Then he would be ready to take the three of them on the semi-sightseeing tour in fifteen minutes."

She focused her attention on the Lady who was with the Elder before they began their adventure. Focusing and observing a little more while watching the lady closely, she noticed the lady only staring at the Elder and not focused about the things around her. The Lady's posture was odd: she did not cringe or turn around as Louise did when a loud bell began ringing from the tower next to the port.

Just then Louise had a thought: ***She wanted to try signing***. Louise remembered it from the past. She went up to the lady and waved in front of her and SIGNED – 'her name was Louise.' "What is your name?" That brought a wide smile to the lady's face, which pleased Louise. She signed back – 'my name is Sollent.'

That was a great breakthrough. The lady was not verbal. Louise instantly signed as best she could to the Lady, what the arrangements entailed.

The lady signed that she brought Euros. Louise, *thanked her lucky stars that she had been polite to the Elder all those days at the beach. She was pleased that she had also shown compassion for Mr. E. She reflected on her insights for not giving up and knew how to use sign language to converse with the lady.*

They had a Semi-Tour booked.

They were not stuck for nine hours.

There was communication with the lady.

The three left-over passengers had four hours to visit the countryside before returning to the MALL. The three passengers went to explore sights outside of the tourist's usual route as soon as the taxi-man had finished eating.

The Elder seemed a bit more relaxed in the small group setting and the guide spoke in the English language. Louise did the signing language to help the lady with the tour sights. While on the touring adventures, the Elder had issues with his camera: Louise assisted.

No mentioning of his knee aches or pain to her. He even beckoned the lady over to have both of their photos taken by the flamboyant tree. They were both grinning like kiddies.

Louise kept counting her blessings for deciding to assist the two leftover passengers. Which in turn worked out better for all. They saw stunning views from above the Capital of the French Capital from different vantage points.

They saw ferries entering and leaving the port from way above the docking site.

They went to Old Forts with cannons and lookout stations from past wars.

They ventured into the historical buildings that depicted the island's history.

They viewed small waterfalls cascading into small pools of water where swans glided smoothly in the protected waters.

They went into the Botanical gardens to appreciate the fauna which bloomed and blossomed in a variety of colours. Unusual fauna and fragrant plants adorned the grounds.

They toured the Governors quarters maintained in colonial splendour.

They Toured the market-place and purchased fruits to eat as they walked the paths.

They saw Historical Churches along the route as they drove along.

The group pleased with the amazing sights and the places they explored, made the best of the short, unexpected tour. With no tour guides, except the pleasant knowledge of the Taxi-man pointing out the features and history along the way, it made up for a shaky beginning.

As the tour was ending, Louise asked the Elder for the Euros to pay the Taxi Driver. Mr. E, did not complain or ask questions. He handed the money to Louise. Louise realized it was more $$$$ than the $70. She took out the $70 plus $10 for a tip and gave the remainder back to Mr. E. She complimented the Taxi-man for the tour before he directed them to the mall.

The three travellers approached the Mall and entered into the cool building to face a long corridor expanding in both directions. To be polite, Louise questioned Mr. E where he would like to begin. "*Going to the left or going the right?*"

The Elder shrugged. Louise, decided not to ask any more questions of him. She should have said, "*Just follow me and let us explore since we are all new to the place.*"

Shopping was the test of nerves and patience for Louise. She had to buffer between the Elder and the Lady by helping with the French Language in the shops. *It was all for a noble cause she kept telling herself. She was in the right place at the right time. She had to pull herself together and do what she had to do by helping the two travelers.*

Rather than argue or cause a confrontation with the Elder when he was indecisive with what to buy in the shops, Louise reminded him that the Ferry was leaving at 5 pm and they had more shops to explore.

Mr. E, claimed he needed to get things for people but had no idea what to get. He seemed frazzled when things were not clear to him. Louise asked if the item was for a female or a male: or young or old: or for what occasion. That made it easier and less pressured for him. Meanwhile, Louise kept including the sign-language for the lady. She had to be fair to both of them.

Eventually, Mr. E and the Lady compared items in different stores and used their Euros to buy souvenirs and gifts. Louise on the other hand, had the good fortune of finding one shop in the Mall that accepted credit cards. *No more worrying about not having Euros.*

Near the end of doubling back and forth to obtain the best prices for their money, the Elder said, his knees were paining him. *You would think that they would hurt him after all the touring and walking for nine hours from shop to shop.*

Louise suggested that they all sit, rest, and eat. After eating and taking a break, the three shopped until it was time to board the ferry back home.

It was finally, five o'clock and the ferry was waiting for everyone to board. The passenger's passports were handed to the individuals with immigration documents to fill out for their return. This gave the Agent the correct count of the people rather than asking whether this person was there or not.

To the passenger's amazement the guide spoiled the happy adventurous day by saying, *You have to pay departure taxes.*

Somehow, they all managed by working together to get the taxes paid in EUROS, of course.

Louise did her magic and signed to the lady and simply told the

Elder that he had pay departure tax. No more asking. To her surprise, he handed her enough money to pay for the three of them. What a miracle indeed!

She collected her passport and found a seat in the back and prepared for her long ride back. She filled out her immigration papers before she settled down for a nap. It had been a long day and it began to get darker as the passengers were all accounted for and seated when the ferry departed the port. The lights dimmed as the Captain announced the safety rules.

Louise was not concerned where the Lady or the Elder sat since the passports were handed out randomly and she had accomplished her honourable deeds for the day.

She helped to secure a decent tour for the Trio.

She maintained the sign-language communications.

She helped with the bargaining prices when they shopped.

She sorted out the taxes for boarding.

As Louise was about to settle into a deep comfortable sleep, she was awoken to "Ladies and Gentlemen We are nearing the Home Port" along with bright lights flashing on and off.

The Agent spoke on the loudspeaker thanking them for the utilizing the Ferry for the trip. She also said that she hoped they had an enjoyable time in Guadeloupe. In addition, she suggested that they looked around their seats to collect their belongings, passports, and documents for faster immigration clearance. The quicker they moved the faster they will get out of the port authority.

It was close to midnight. The Immigration staff were working overtime for the late ferry arrival as the agent mentioned.

Various passengers gathered to wait for the opening of the door. Louise thought that her back seat would have made it easier to exit first. Others had the same idea in mind. She looked ahead at the pathway to the Customs Building, ready to get off and get into the building to clear customs. She did not have any alcohol to declare. It would be an easy clearing in the customs office.

Louise was not the first one out of the door that evening. She stepped off the ferry and looked up ahead on the path towards the

Immigration building that was open and lit up brightly. Just then she spotted through her sleepy eyes someone tall moving as though in a race running a 100m dash. Another person in a dress was a close pace behind.

'They sure were in a hurry,' Louise thought.

All of a sudden, she spotted the Lady with whom she helped by signing. She waved to her with sleepy eyes and signed, "*Where was the Elder?*" The lady signed that he was one of the two figures moving up the path.

Louise rubbed her eyes, focused better, and laughed inside. So that was his agenda each day at the beach as well as this trip. What a sight!

The Elder who complained of aches and pains in the day found a lady at night with whom he could entertain and forget about his pain.

MR. SWEET THE D.O.M

"I dare you to climb the tree and pick SIR DOM's peaches," Pierre said to his brother Pascual.

"No way I am going in his yard: you go," said Pascual. "I am not going on Mr. DOM's property even if he has the sweetest and plumpest peaches in Apple Valley." "Grams says that all the time."

Pierre pushed Pascual forward, and announced, "Yes you are going to walk up the path, find that peach tree, and pick some peaches for Grand-Ma to bake for the Pie Contest. I will be your look out."

SIR DOM had the only peach tree this side of the county. Apple Valley was known for Apples, of course. The peach tree was not visible to anyone passing along the road.

'SIR DOM' as the boys called the man, a title given by the local boys based on his appearance when he went to the local store. They only knew that he acted grumpy and kept to himself. Local kids were too afraid to enter onto his property.

"Well, why do you not go and pick them yourself." "Stop pushing me so hard. Not because I am on the soccer team, does not mean I have to be the one to go and pick the peaches. You are on the team too," his brother stated.

"I am the eldest," said Pierre. "I am telling you that Grand-Ma wants to win this year at the Pie festival. I know that she was fed up with the Church ladies winning the prizes last year."

"You know that; and I know that too!" said, Pascual enthusiastically. "There was more to Apple Valley than Apples. This year I hope that her Secret Apple Pie will be the talk of the Valley. It was time for a change. Grannie should be the one to be on that magazine." "She made excellent pies, tarts, strudels, and cobblers."

Pascual recalled last year at the annual fair, the first, second and third place winners had their photos in the Southern Living Magazine.

To top it off, the winner won a trip to England and visited the Queen. This year the trip was a trip to Italy and a chance to cook with the famous Chef, Buona-Tartellini.

Pascual pushed back and replied, “You are not the eldest and you are on the soccer team too.” Pierre quickly retorted, “I am just the goalie: I only block the balls coming into the net. You are the fastest and best goal scorer.” Pierre and Pascual were triplets. Princess their sister, was the eldest. The trio were eight years of age.

“Here comes Princess said Pierre with her cart.” “Let us ask her to get some peaches for Grand-Ma Baker.”

“That is not a cart, it her doll carriage,” said Pascual.

Pierre, brushed him out of the way and said, “I am going to tell her that Grannie told her to pick some peaches. Do you know that Grams said that SIR DOM guards his peach trees like a fox?”

“How could he guard like a fox? Foxes do not guard. Dogs do; and they bark, and I do not see or hear any dogs,” said Pascual.

“That is why he uses foxes. They do not bark,” said Pierre.

“She is coming closer,” Pascual said, “I will ask her. You are too pushy.” “Hello little sister, are you coming to help us?”

Princess looked skeptically at her troublesome brothers and gave them a quizzical look. “What tricks are you two up to today?,” she inquired sweetly?

“Well, we have to pick peaches for grannie’s pie contest, and we want you to use your doll carriage to sneak in and carry the peaches from SIR DOM’s tree,” said Pascual. “We know that you are the only one to touch your carriage, so we are asking you to go in and pick them.”

Princess rolled her eyes at the boys and walked pass them, opened the gate and looked back and said, “His name is not SIR DOM. His name is Mr. Sweet. Why do you boys call him SIR DOM?”

Pierre pushed out his chest and said, “He is not sweet. His nickname means Dirty Old Man – DOM.”

Their sister nicely informed them, “If you work in your garden all day, you will get Dirty. He is Older than us, and he is a Man. Be nice.” “Shall I call you both BAIT?”

Pascual asked, “What is that?”

She grinned: "Boys Always In Trouble."

Princess pouted her lips and blew a kiss to her two brothers and daintily closed the gate and gracefully walked up the path.

The boy's mouths dropped in unison at her explanation, as she regally walked up the path to Mr. Sweets ranch house. They gazed at her in awe: they were too afraid to venture boldly as their sister did.

"That is why she is the eldest," Pascual said, as he stuck out his tongue at Pierre.

Princess sashayed up the path and glided over to the verandah and looked around to see Mr. Sweet rocking in his chair. She batted her eyes and said, "Hello Mr. Sweet, Grannie sends her blessings and asked me to get peaches for her pie contest. She sent empty jars and bottles, Lemon juice she squeezed from her lemons, red and yellow apples, and fresh bread she baked especially for you."

Mr. Sweet eyes watered sadly before he spoke. "I will make some lemonade from the juice and enjoy the fresh bread. Please thank her for me when you get back home. How is she these days"

"She is doing well Sir, and very keen on winning this year's pie contest. Your peaches she told me will be her secret advantage." Mr. Sweet, listened to Little Princess as she chatted about her grannie wanting to win the contest and especially, about the escapades her brothers were getting into.

Mr. Sweet's face looked melancholy, yet his eyes focused on her, as he hung unto every word she uttered. (He secretly lifted out the note that was at the bottom of the basket under the lemon juice).

Princess was happy to chat with Mr. Sweet because she knew no one wanted to visit him and he never told her she talked too much. Mr. Sweet advised her to begin writing a journal. She perked up even more as he handed her a little black book with blank lines.

Reluctantly, Mr. Sweet got up from his chair and asked her to walk with him to his prized peach tree. He could listen to her all day. She was a happy child and sure of herself. If only the boys would visit, he thought to himself, smiling tenderly, as they walked to the peach tree.

Princess saw barbed wires, small trees with thorns and strange looking traps around the tree. Under the tree limbs a net hung to catch the peaches as they fell. She thought that was a smart idea and made a mental note to write in her journal. This is why the boys were afraid to come and pick the peaches? Therefore, she would advise them it was not safe to pick peaches without asking: They were her brothers!

Mr. Sweet asked princess to wait by the edge of the path while he went into his fortress behind the tree and brought out a bucket of peaches for her. He had everything figured out to keep the peaches peachy and not bruised or blemished. When he exited from his maze, he filled her carriage with huge jars of jam, bottle of juice and gave her a wagon filled with peaches in a box to keep them safe on her walk home.

"Please go straight home with the peaches to keep them fresh, my Little Princess. Keep the wagon from rocking too much and no running," Mr. Sweet warned her.

With her twinkling green eyes that looked familiar to him, she merrily thanked him for the book, the peaches, and the talk. "What will you do with the rest of the peaches, Mr. Sweet?"

Smiling tenderly, he said, "My dear princess I will make more jams, and lots of juice. I added two extra jams in your wagon for your grannie. Her name written on the extra jars. Please tell her it is a special batch."

Little did Princess know that Mr. Sweet was making Wine not juice. Under the box of peaches was another box with Peach Wine. Grannie was providing him with the lime juice, apples (the secret ingredient), and empty jars to keep him in business.

Princess whistled to herself and gently pulled the wagon down the path and out of the gate towards her brothers.

Pierre and Pascual with a lighter shade of green eyes stood mesmerized seeing her with her bounty of peaches in the wagon. They could not find the words to ask her how she picked the peaches so quickly. Princess continued walking gracefully and continued to whistle, without speaking to them.

Pierre pulled her pigtail as she strolled pass him. She spun around and scowled at him, gave him one look as if to say, 'I dare you to do that again.' He knew that look and refrained from assessing his luck a second time.

Pascual reached into the wagon and grabbed a peach. Princess twisted around and glared at him and said, "I am going to count to two. If that peach in not gently placed back into that wagon, you will not be sleeping in your bed tonight."

Pascual, have never seen her that fierce before. He laid the peach gently back into the wagon as if it was an egg.

Princess pirouetted smoothly and began to whistle again as she gently pulled the wagon behind her to grannie's house. The two boys sulked along the road behind the wagon in complete silence not daring to even to whisper to each other.

When the trio arrived at grannie's house, she waited eagerly for princess to pull the wagon up the path. Her eyes were sparkling radiantly with glee and her face was ablaze with a smile of pure joy. The boys thought that she was thinking of winning the pie contest at the festival. However, she was thinking of what was under the box of peaches and the peaches of course.

Looking sternly at Pierre and Pascual, Grand-Ma Baker said, "Here is a bag for each of you. You both know what to do."

"Get a move on it."

I am baking your favourite turnovers today. You both know what I need. The boys knew that the apples from their Grand-Ma's garden was the goal set for them. (They will pick and fill their bags). They loved grannie's apple turnovers.

In a firm voice, Grand-Ma spoke directly to Pierre. "Make certain that you pick the apples from the Red tree." She did not have to tell Pascual what he needed to do. Chuckling aloud, Grannie knew that both boys would compete with each other to pick the apples for her. If any of the apples had bruises or blemishes, Grand-Ma Baker would not make any apple turnovers. Grannie knew the brother's cooperation would be 100 percent because she used right tone of voice. The duo of the triplets would not deviate from her directives. Just as their sister did when she visited Mr. Sweet; the boys went on her Apple picking mission and would execute that mission without failing.

'That would keep them occupied for a while.' Grand-Ma smiled to herself and hoped it was enough time for her to sit and hear about the little girl's journey to Mr. Sweet. "Now, Now, my sweet angel," she remarked to Princess. "Did he find the note under the lemon juice?"

Blushing shyly, Princess answered, "Yes, Grand-Ma. He did find the note and his eyes were teary and sparkling." "Did you send him sad news grannie?"

"No, no dearie. I sent him a note to let him know what was progressing with his investments. (Grand-Ma's note detailed more than the investments.)"

She was his distributer for the Peach Wine. The buyers for the wine on the open market were in France, Spain, and Portugal. Mr. Sweet's main focus was distribution of his new wine to the Italian restaurant industry. It was also one of the main reason Grand-Ma Baker hoped to win the contest at the festival. Another reason was to have her baked deserts served in the Italian restaurants.

"Oh," said Princess, "That was so nice of you, grannie. He told me to tell you that two of the Jars had your name and they were a special batch. He also gave me a journal to record my adventures and record your recipes. One day I will be famous."

"My dear Princess, you are already famous. You just do not even know it as yet."

Meanwhile, as they washed and pealed the peaches Grand-Ma and Princess chatted and shared what transpired on her trip to pick the peaches. Grand-Ma was sure asking lots of questions about Mr. Sweet today. Princess wondered if grannie was sweet on Mr. Sweet! Her eyes shone whenever she asked about him. She was about to ask grannie a question when the boys arrived with their apples. Pascual with the yellow apples and Pierre with the red ones.

Just as Princess was about to say something to grannie, the triplets mother walked in with to help with the preparations for the BIG WIN. "Why are you two staring at the apples like that? Get the peelers. The apples will not peel themselves," her mom chided.

Once again, the Princess' moment faded. She fumed silently and kept peeling her Peaches. 'Just you wait she told herself, I am going to get my chance to talk.'

Princess did not get a chance to have her talk with Grand-Ma due to the hustle and bustle and preparations for the Festival. It was Grand-Ma's time to shine. She did not want to spoil Grams chances with her chattering or inquisitive questions.

Her mom tried to get her talking about her day peach picking, but Princess focused on her pealing and prepping for the pies. She kept her emerald, green eyes on her brothers as they peeled their apples. Her fiery piercing and staring eyes kept them synchronized and on-task. No wonder she was the first born. Her eyes commanded respect without words.

Festival day! It was the day Grand-Ma Baker was waiting for. The team worked through the night. They baked the pies tirelessly all day and into the early morning without resting. The triplets went to bed early, while Grannie added the secret ingredients Mr. Sweet had sent with Princess. The key was his cultivated hybrid peaches! Mr. Sweet added Grand-Ma's hybrid apples to elevate the texture and flavour in his Peach wine.

When the sun began to peek over the horizon, the team plopped down on the sofa for a short nap. Grand-Ma shook the sleep from her eyes and silently slipped out of the house. The workload was complete. It was Presentation Pie Day at the town hall at noon. Princess and the boys awoke to a house filled with mouth warming aromas of apples and peaches wharfing in their noses. No doubt what delicious delights they would eat for breakfast when they sat down. Princess hoped that her mom did not ask her to go home with the boys. She wanted to stay with Grand-Ma until the festival began in the afternoon. There was so much she wanted to ask her grannie.

"Grand-Ma Baker where are you? Grand-Ma Baker?" She heard her mom announcing downstairs.

Princess went to Grand-Ma's door and knocked. "Grannie, Grannie, are you awake? It was the day you waited for."

With silence on the other side of the door. She squeezed the handle and tiptoed into the room. Grand-Ma Baker was not in her room. Strange, princess thought.

"Mom, she is not upstairs" Princess called downstairs as she hurried down to have a scrumptious meal. Curious, that her grannie was not in the kitchen, she screwed up her face, twirled her pigtails, and watched her brothers sitting at the table.

With thoughts swirling in her head, she suddenly lost her appetite even though the smells were tempting. Her grannie was not visible to talk to.

Honey, "What is wrong? You love Grand-Ma's fritters and waffles," her mom was saying.

To Princess, her mons voice sounded far away.

"Nothing, nothing," Princess piped up. "What time is it please?" Her mom said, "It is time for you to eat and then run home to change into your outfit for the festival. It is ten in the morning."

Princess morning passed in a blur as she had unsettling thoughts swirling around in her mind. Her brothers wrestling in the yard, yelling at each other, and running after the new puppy did not interrupt her worrying. The trucks came by with the inspectors as they labelled the pies and marked the boxes. Her mom did all of the supervision and guarded the prized pies. Still no visible sign of her Grannie. Princess stonily watched the process like a robot. Where was her grannie?

Her brothers quieted down and raced inside when their sister was not outside chasing them around. Pierre pulled her hair, and she did not snap like a turtle or reprimand him. As Pascual's was about to reach out to give her a dirty hug, a welcoming voice sounded,

"Boys? Look at you two. Why is it you are both so dirty?" Grannie voice directed at them, with her hand on her hip. Princess startled out of her trance and automatically chimed in,

"Now look at the two DCB?"

Pierre squinting up his face said, "DCB?"

"Dirt Covered Boys," said Princess as she folded her arms and tapped her feet. "I bet you both would not like it if the entire town called you by that name. Well, SIR DOM does not like that either.re town called you by that name."

Her grannie was back. Not fretting about asking where she was all morning, she ran to hug her grannie with shining eyes that sparkled and fluttered.

"Double Trouble P, get yourselves bathed and dressed as fast as you can and be ready when the motor cage arrives." Both boys jumped and turned at a familiar voice to see Mr. Sweet at the door. He was looking dapper and spotless for a DOM. Almost unrecognizable and cleaned shaved. Princess looked as if someone was shaking her as her head bobbed up and down in laughter. "Chop, Chop, Double T. P," she chuckled as both boys scampered upstairs.

Mr. Sweet, laughed and had eyes only for Grand-Ma Baker. "I am here to help with the transporting of the Jams and Pies for the festival. Let us get these pies and Jams to the Town Hall and win this prize."

Princess was thinking along the same thoughts when a well-dressed regal gentlemen waltzed through the kitchen. He saluted Mr. Sweet and said, "Duke Phillip, the royal motor car will be arriving in an hour. The unmarked van is ready for us to load the pies to the fair. Will you be needing anything else before the motor carriage arrives?"

For the second time in the day Princess could not say anything. Did she imagine what she heard? Did they just call Mr. Sweet, Duke Phillip? While her mind was reeling with the new overwhelming news, she swooned and then she opened her eyes to see her Grand-Ma fanning her with a kitchen towel.

"What, What, I am fine," she replied, as she refocused her foggy thoughts. Princess realized it was not grannie looking at her. It was Mr. Sweet, or Duke Sweet or Duke Phillip? Which one was it? She was so confused.

"Yes, sir. What do I call you? Sir Sweet Duke? Or Mr. Duke Phillip? Or Mr. Duke Sweet?"

The Duke looked into Princess eyes that looked so much like his brother's eyes and laughed, "I will tell you what. How about calling me Uncle Phillip? I am really the Duke-Of-Manchnant."

Little Princess's eyes widened in bewilderment of what the Duke just shared with her. Her sharp mind was churning as she grinned with glee at her new thoughts. Meanwhile she began twirling around the kitchen like a ballet dancer and giggled, spun, and sang, "The boys were correct: they were right to call you a DOM, but so wrong at the same time. Yes you are The – DOM – The Duke-Of-Manchnant."

Watching her with pride he realized how much her infectious smile radiated from her face melted his heart. He could not help but to pull her into his arms. Tears flowed freely from his eyes as he told her, "We will be seeing lots of each other: but for now, I have another important thing to tell you and the boys."

As if on cue, who should walk down the stairs all rosy and clean and freshly dressed? The two boys.

"Come on boys, come this way. Please do not be sacred. I am not a fox, and I will not hurt you. What I have to share concerns the three of you."

Both boys hesitantly moved closer towards their sister who was hopping from one foot to the other and as if she had to go to the toilet. They looked at their sister and glanced at Grand-Ma Baker who was crying.

Pascual whispered, "We are in serious trouble now. Grannie never cries."

Pierre blurted out, "I told her to get those peaches. We are so sorry SIR DOM."

Princess heard those three letters spoken by her brother she fell on the floor and rolled around shouting, "He is a DOM. He is a DOM." Both boys cringed simultaneously with guilty looks and lowered their heads in shame while retreating slowly into a corner.

The man they called Sir DOM looked at them with a twinkling smile, inviting arms outstretched, beckoning them to get closer towards him. Pascual shyly approached the man while gripping his brother's hand for support and glancing suspiciously at Princess. SIR DOM did not look angry or sad.

SIR DOM revealed to them that their mother was not a relative of theirs and neither was Grand-Ma Baker their grandmother. She was his partner (and more) in the new Wine and Pastry Business.

Apparently, The Duke resided in the City in the off season and stayed in the country before and during the harvesting. He commuted from the town to the country to cultivate and harvest the fruits from the Hybrid Peach tree. Along with Ms. Bakers' Hybrid Apple trees products, both of them had established a unique combination of Vintage wine and flavourful desserts fit for royalty.

He lovingly reflected on the rebuilding of his family's name and to restore the fortune which his deceased brother had squandered. His ultimate quest: Starting a family of his own and getting reacquainted with the triplets to give them a loving home.

When obstacles deter your plans, or failures slow your progress: Motivate yourself in a different direction and restart with new goals in mind.

BEAUTY UNFOLDED

When Beauty rises
In the light,
Felt, and embraced,
But elusive.
It is seen.

Beauty not recognized
Immediately,
Is reflected
Visualized
And shared.

When Beauty is invisible
It becomes unreachable
You become unsure
Insecure
Searching for more.

If Beauty escapes
In passing,
It will diffuse
Leaving behind
A beautiful glow
Giving one Hope.

A DAY IN THE LIFE OF A CUP

BY YOUNG NICOLE L. BOATSWAIN

One day in a store a little cup stood on a shelf waiting to be bought. All of his little cup friends and family were being bought by the dozens. One day the little cup was bought and travelled home with his family. When he got home they poured hot liquid into him then they left him in a sink of dirty dishes and did not wash him. Finally, when they got to washing him they dropped him and broke him. They then decided to glue him back together with cheap glue which started to fall apart. So, the family just threw him away like a piece of trash. And that was the end of the little cup. Nobody knew what happened to him after that. That poor little cup was gone forever.

THE END

www.ingramcontent.com/pod-product-compliance
Lightning Source LLC
Chambersburg PA
CBHW021749190726
48290CB00008B/2541

9781736622612